FOO

Story • Richard Thompson   Art • Eugenie Fernandes

Annick Press   Toronto, Canada

When Jesse was two she learned about blowing kisses.

She would kiss her hand, and while the kiss was still warm and light, she would blow as hard as she could, "FOO."

She foo-ed kisses to all her friends, to her Auntie Aleta and to the lady at the popsicle store.

She foo-ed kisses to puppies and kittens and Ben's pet worms. Everybody liked her foo kisses.

She foo-ed a kiss to the sun when it was going down. The sun was so happy, it made the whole sky glow pink and orange.

She foo-ed a kiss to the moon. The moon liked it so much, it followed her home and hung in the branches of a tree outside her window, waiting for another.

She foo-ed a kiss to a summer cloud after the rain had stopped. The summer cloud was so tickled, it spread a rainbow right across the sky.

She foo-ed a kiss to a winter cloud. The cloud's cold heart was melted just a little bit, and it dropped a million tiny snow kisses through the sky.

She foo-ed a kiss to a train. The train was so surprised, it blew its whistle twice, really loudly.

She foo-ed a kiss to a bee. The bee buzzed right over to tell a flower all about it.

She foo-ed a kiss to the river. The river was very pleased, and it gurgled softly to her.

She foo-ed lots of kisses to her dad. He liked her kisses so much, he always came right over and gave her a great big hug.

But nobody liked her foo kisses more than her mom…

One evening Jesse's mom said, "Oh, I don't feel like going to dance class tonight, I'm just too tired."

Jesse didn't want her to go either.

"I guess I'd better," her mom finally said, and she went.

That evening Jesse's dad helped her put on her jammies and brushed her teeth for her. He read her two stories, and snuggled her in his arms.

But Jesse couldn't go to sleep.

"I want my mommy," she said.

"Your mommy will be home soon," said her dad. "When she gets home she will come and give you a kiss goodnight."

"I want to kiss her now," said Jesse.

"Jesse, your mommy isn't here right now," said her dad. He thought for a while. Then he said, "You could send her a foo kiss."

Jesse unsnuggled herself and smiled. "Okay," she said.

Her daddy opened the window a crack, and Jesse blew two big kisses—"Foo, Foo,"— out into the night. The kisses sailed away and disappeared in the dark.

Jesse settled back into her dad's arms and fell asleep.

The kisses sailed across the city. They cast little kiss shadows under the street lamps. They sailed past windows and peeked in to see families watching TV or playing games or doing the supper dishes.

The kisses flew on through the night until they got to the school where Jesse's mom did her dancing. They slipped in through a crack between the doors, and drifted for a long time, until they heard music, and came to the dancing room. Jesse's mom was there, but she wasn't dancing.

She was standing with her arms folded, watching the other dancers making fancy shapes with their bodies, running on their tiptoes, twirling.

The foo kisses landed softly on her cheek. All of a sudden, Jesse's mom felt like dancing after all. She unfolded her arms and started to twirl on her tiptoes, around and around.

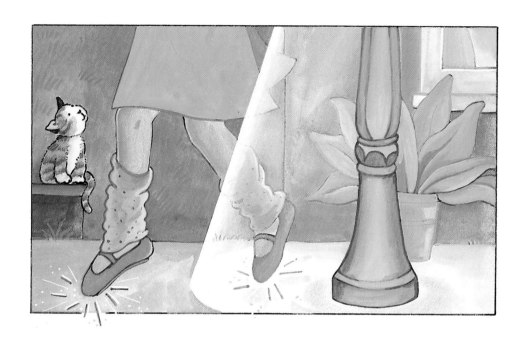

All the way home, the good tiptoe feeling stayed with her.

And when she got home, the first thing she did was go to Jesse's room and give her back her kisses.

Fourth printing, February 1992

Annick Press

Graphic realization and
design by Eugenie Fernandes

Annick Press gratefully acknowledges
the support of The Canada Council
and The Ontario Arts Council

Canadian Cataloguing in Publication Data

Thompson, Richard, 1951–
  Foo

(The Jesse adventures)
1st ed.
ISBN 1-55037-005-7 (bound) ISBN 1-55037-004-9 (pbk.)

I. Fernandes, Eugenie, 1951–   . II. Title.
III. Series: Thompson, Richard, 1951–   . The
Jesse adventures.

PS8589.H65F66 1988   jC813'.54   C87-095182-3
PZ7.T46Fo 1988

Distributed in Canada and the USA by:
Firefly Books Ltd.,
250 Sparks Avenue
North York, Ontario
M2H 2S4

Printed and bound in Canada
by D.W Friesen & Sons Ltd.